merry Christmas, Avi!

with love from mom & Dad

Christmas, 1989

JUST ENOUGH IS PLENTY
A HANUKKAH TALE

JUST ENOUGH IS PLENTY
A HANUKKAH TALE

BY BARBARA DIAMOND GOLDIN
PAINTINGS BY SEYMOUR CHWAST

VIKING KESTREL

The artwork was rendered with acrylic paint on canvas board.

VIKING KESTREL
Published by the Penguin Group
Viking Penguin Inc., 40 West 23rd Street, New York, New York 10010, U.S.A.
Penguin Books Ltd, 27 Wrights Lane, London W8 5TZ England
Penguin Books Australia Ltd, Ringwood, Victoria, Australia
Penguin Books Canada Ltd, 2801 John Street, Markham, Ontario, Canada L3R 1B4
Penguin Books (N.Z.) Ltd, 182–190 Wairau Road, Auckland 10, New Zealand

Penguin Books Ltd, Registered Offices: Harmondsworth, Middlesex, England

First published in 1988 by Viking Penguin Inc.
Published simultaneously in Canada

Library of Congress Cataloging in Publication Data
Goldin, Barbara Diamond   Just enough is plenty: a Hanukkah tale
by Barbara Diamond Goldin; illustrated by Seymour Chwast.   p. cm.
Summary: With Hanukkah about to begin, Malka is worried because
her family is so poor, but when a poor stranger comes to the door,
her generous family cannot turn him away.
ISBN 0-670-81852-6
[1. Hanukkah—Fiction. 2. Jews—Fiction.] I. Chwast, Seymour, ill. II. Title.
PZ7.G5674Ju 1988   [E]—dc 19   88-3953   CIP
Color separations by Imago Ltd., Hong Kong
Printed in Hong Kong by South China Printing Company
Set in Bookman

1 2 3 4 5 92 91 90 89 88

Dedicated to my parents, Anne and Mort Diamond, who have given me love, support, and an appreciation for my heritage.

B.D.G.

Malka's family lived in a village in Poland. They were poor, but not so poor. They had candles for the Sabbath, noisemakers for Purim, and spinning tops for Hanukkah.

Mama was busy preparing for tonight, the first of the eight nights of Hanukkah. She peeled onions and grated potatoes for the latkes, the potato pancakes.

Malka's younger brother Zalman carved a dreidel, a spinning top.

"This dreidel will spin the fastest of all," he boasted.

Papa was working long hours in his tailor shop so they could buy more food for the holiday. More potatoes, more onions, more flour, more oil.

For on the first night of Hanukkah, Malka's family always invited many guests. But this year only Aunt Hindy and Uncle Shmuel were coming to visit.

"Only two guests?" Malka asked. "Last year, we had so many guests that Papa had to put boards over the pickle barrels to make the table big enough."

"That was last year," Mama said gently. "This year has not been a good one for Papa in the shop. People bring him just a little mending here, a little mending there. He cannot afford to buy new material to sew fancy holiday dresses and fine suits."

"But it's Hanukkah," Malka reminded Mama.

Mama patted Malka's shoulder. "Don't worry, Malkaleh. We know how to stretch. We're poor, but not so poor. Now go. Ask Papa if he has a few more coins. I need more eggs for the latkes."

Malka bundled up in her jacket and shawl, her scarf and boots. It was cold and snowy and so windy. The wind chased her all the way to the marketplace.

She raced into Papa's shop. "Mama sent me to buy more eggs."

"More eggs. More this, more that. Soon there will be no kopeks left. Not even one for Hanukkah money."

Malka stood still in the doorway. No Hanukkah money! Was Papa joking? How could she and Zalman play the dreidel game without even a kopek?

"Malka, don't just stand there. Here. Go buy the eggs," Papa said. "And quickly. Aunt Hindy and Uncle Shmuel will be here soon."

The coins that Papa gave her for the eggs jingled inside her pocket as she ran.

Clink. Clink.

Last year, Malka used her Hanukkah money to buy candy treats at the marketplace and sleigh rides around the village.

Clink. Clink.

But this was egg money.

Malka carried the eggs carefully back to the house. She burst into tears when she saw Mama. "Papa doesn't even have a kopek left for us," she wailed. "No Hanukkah money."

"Did Papa say that?"

Malka nodded. Her chin quivered and she couldn't say another word.

Mama wiped her hands on her apron and hugged Malka close. "Was there ever a Hanukkah without a kopek for a child to play dreidel with?"

Malka shrugged. She didn't know.

Suddenly, there were loud noises at the door: horses whinnying and stomping and people shouting, "Happy Hanukkah!"

"It's them!" Mama cried. "And the latkes aren't fried yet." She ran to the door to welcome Aunt Hindy and Uncle Shmuel, and then she hurried back into the kitchen to fry latkes.

When she finished, she put a coin in the charity box on the shelf, just as she did before each holiday and Sabbath. Malka saw her.

"What if that's our last kopek?" Malka whispered to Zalman.

Then Papa came in from the shop, and the whole family gathered around the little brass menorah on the windowsill.

Papa picked up the *shammash,* the special candle at the top of the menorah, and chanted the familiar prayers. "Blessed is God who commanded us to light the Chanukah candles. . . . Blessed is God who worked miracles for our ancestors long ago . . ."

Zalman tugged at Malka's sleeve. "What miracles?" he asked in a whisper.

"You remember. The oil in the Temple. The oil that burned for eight days instead of only one," Malka explained quickly.

When Papa finished the blessings, he used the *shammash* to light the first candle in the menorah. The other seven candle-holders were empty, waiting for their turn on the nights to come.

"Sit down, everyone," Mama said, and rushed into the kitchen.

Malka carried platters of latkes to the table as soon as Mama filled them. She saw Papa give Zalman the warning eye as Zalman piled six latkes on his plate.

Papa came into the kitchen. "Is there enough?' he whispered to Mama.

"Just enough," said Mama.

When Malka put the last latke on the table, she and Papa and Mama sat down, too.

There was a knock on the door.

"Did you invite anyone else?" asked Mama.

"No," said Papa. He got up to see who was there.

It was a peddler with a large sack on his back. He had white hair and wore a wrinkled black greatcoat and torn boots.

"I saw the Hanukkah lights in your window." He spoke softly with his head bowed.

Mama stood up and went to the door. "Come in. Join us. Just like Abraham and Sarah in the Bible, we always have something for the stranger who knocks on our door."

Papa gave Mama a worried look. So did Malka. "We can stretch the 'just enough,' " Mama whispered to them. "We're poor, but not so poor."

Mama gave the old man one of her latkes. So did Papa. So did Malka, Aunt Hindy, Uncle Shmuel and even Zalman.

Everyone ate the latkes with apple sauce and sour cream.

"I'm finished, Papa," said Zalman. "Can I play dreidel?"

"Dreidel. I haven't played dreidel in years." The old man leaned forward and beckoned Zalman closer with his finger. "Do you have one?"

"The fastest one in my class," Zalman said.

The old man looked at Papa. "I have a few kopeks. The children could use them to play the dreidel game."

Malka was glad and thanked the peddler. Now she would have a kopek to play with. But still no candy treats or sleigh rides. No cousins or friends to fill the house.

Malka and Zalman sat on the floor. So did the old man. He took turns with the dreidel, too.

Spin.

Shin. Put one in the pile.

Twirl.

Hay. Take half the coins.

Spin again.

Nun. Take nothing.

Twirl again.

Gimmel. Take all.

Just like the children, the old man made a face when the top landed on *nun*, nothing, and he laughed when the top stopped on *gimmel*, take all.

Then he taught the children songs with words that went around and around again. Once he sang the words loudly and happily, and once he hummed the tune quietly with his eyes closed. *Oy chiri biri biri bim bum bum, Oy chiri biri biri bim bum bum*. Still singing, he grabbed their hands and they danced in circles, whirling like dreidels themselves.

Giggling and huffing, Malka and Zalman fell to the floor.

The old man reached into his peddler's sack and drew out one book and then another. He read the stories in his soft voice. Some of them made Malka laugh, others brought tears to her eyes. His stories were about kind people and cruel people, about angels and wonder-working rabbis, about beggars and miracles.

Of all the stories, her favorites were the ones about Elijah the Prophet, who would come back to earth to help someone who was poor but kindhearted. One time Elijah dressed as a horseman, one time as a beggar, one time as a magician.

"It's as if the whole house were filled with guests," Malka told the peddler. "With the people of your stories."

Later that night, after Aunt Hindy and Uncle Shmuel left, Papa made a sleeping place for the peddler. He piled straw by the stove.

Before they went to sleep, the old man gave each child a kopek to keep.

"For your Hanukkah money," he said. "For some candy treats and sleigh rides around the village."

Malka laughed. "How did you know?"

The peddler smiled. "I know."

Then Malka and Zalman tumbled into their beds along one of the kitchen walls.

"Good night, Reb . . . Oh, I don't even know your name," Malka said.

"I'll tell you tomorrow," the old man answered.

When Malka awoke in the morning, she lay
still in her bed, remembering her dreams about
cruel kings and kind farmers, about the people
in the peddler's stories.

"I especially liked the stories about Elijah," Malka
said softly, hoping the old man was awake, too.
But when she looked for him, she saw an empty
pile of straw. He was gone.

"Mama! Papa! Zalman!" Malka called. "Come
quickly. The peddler is gone."

She thought of the winter wind pushing him
down the street.

"Oh, I wish he had stayed. Didn't he know Mama
can always make plenty out of just enough?"
she said to Zalman, who looked disappointed,
too. "And we don't even know his name."

"But wait," Mama said. "What's that over there?
Did he forget something?"

Malka saw the peddler's sack by the door and
ran over to it.

"There's a note," she said. "Mama, what does it
say?"

"Just 'Happy Hanukkah. This will help you,' "
Mama read.

"No name?"

"No. No name."

Malka peeked into the sack. She recognized the book on top. It was the old book with the stories about Elijah.

Malka gasped.

Clutching the book, she turned to Mama and Papa and Zalman. "I know who the peddler is. He's Elijah!"

"Elijah? You really believe that old man is Elijah the Prophet? Oy," Papa said, hitting his head with his hand.

"He could be, Papa," Malka said. "Remember how Elijah left things for the people he visited in those stories?"

"But we are real people, not story-people, Malkaleh. And why would he leave us his whole sackful of books? I'm a tailor, not a book peddler."

Papa turned to the sack. He took out one book after the other, big books and little books, old books and new books. About halfway down the sack, Papa stopped. He stood up, confused.

"There's a problem?" Mama asked anxiously.

"No, not a problem," Papa said hesitantly. "Just . . ."

Once again he stooped down over the sack. They all crowded around him as he lifted one, two, three bolts of silk and more out of the sack. Purple silk, green silk, dotted silk, silk with stripes and checks and flowers.

"Look what your Elijah gave us this Hanukkah!" Papa said to Malka and twirled her happily in the air. "What fancy holiday dresses and fine suits I can make now."

He took Malka's hand and Malka took Zalman's hand and Zalman reached over for Mama.

Malka turned to Mama and said, "I'm glad you're so good at making just enough be plenty!"

Laughing, they all began to dance, and sing,

Oy chiri biri biri bim bum bum,
Oy chiri biri biri bim bum bum,
Oy chiri biri biri bim.

About This Book

Hanukkah, also called the Festival of Lights or the Feast of Dedication, is an eight-day holiday that begins on the 25th of the Hebrew month of Kislev (November or December). It commemorates the successful fight for religious freedom by a small army of Jews more than 2,100 years ago. Judah the Maccabee was their leader against the mighty Syrian-Greek army of Antiochus IV.

After their victory in the hills of Judea, the small Maccabean army recaptured Jerusalem. There they rededicated the desecrated Temple to the worship of God. The Rabbis tell a story about the Maccabees, that they intended to light the Temple's great lamp, the seven-branched menorah. However, they could find only a single jar of sacred oil, enough to last for just one day. Miraculously, this oil burned for eight days—until new oil could be prepared.

To remember the miracle of the Maccabees' victory and the jar of oil that burned for eight days, Jews everywhere light menorahs during Hanukkah. Each of these special lamps, more accurately called a *Hanukkiyah,* holds eight candles, in addition to the *shammash.* This special candle, which is used to light the others, is separate and often higher than the rest.

On the first night of the holiday, the *shammash* is used to light one candle. On the second night, the *shammash* lights two candles, and so on for the eight nights. To proclaim the miracles, it is customary to place the lamps on a windowsill for all to see.

A traditional food eaten on Hanukkah is *latkes,* small potato pancakes, fried in oil, another reminder of the miracle of the oil in the Temple.

Children especially have a good time on Hanukkah. They collect money and gifts from parents and relatives, and play games with a *dreidel* (pronounced "dráy-d'l"), a four-sided top. Using raisins, coins, or nuts, the children each take an equal number of objects and place the rest in a central pile or "pot." They take turns spinning the dreidel. If it lands on the Hebrew letter *nun,* they take nothing from the pot. If it lands on *gimmel,* they take everything from the pot. *Hay* means the player takes half, and *shin* means the player shares or puts one from his pile into the pot. The letters *nun, gimmel, hay,* and *shin* are the first letters of the Hebrew words that mean "A Great Miracle Happened There." And so the game, as well as the food and the lights, serve as reminders of the miracles of the first Hanukkah.

The children who lived in the *shtetl,* the small towns and villages of Eastern Europe at the turn of the century, did not receive gifts on Hanukkah, but they did enjoy many of the other customs that are still practiced. And they, too, retold stories about the heroism of the Maccabees, the rededication of the holy Temple, and the rekindling of the lights of joy and freedom in Jerusalem long ago, just as Jews all over the world do today.